Alef is for Ima

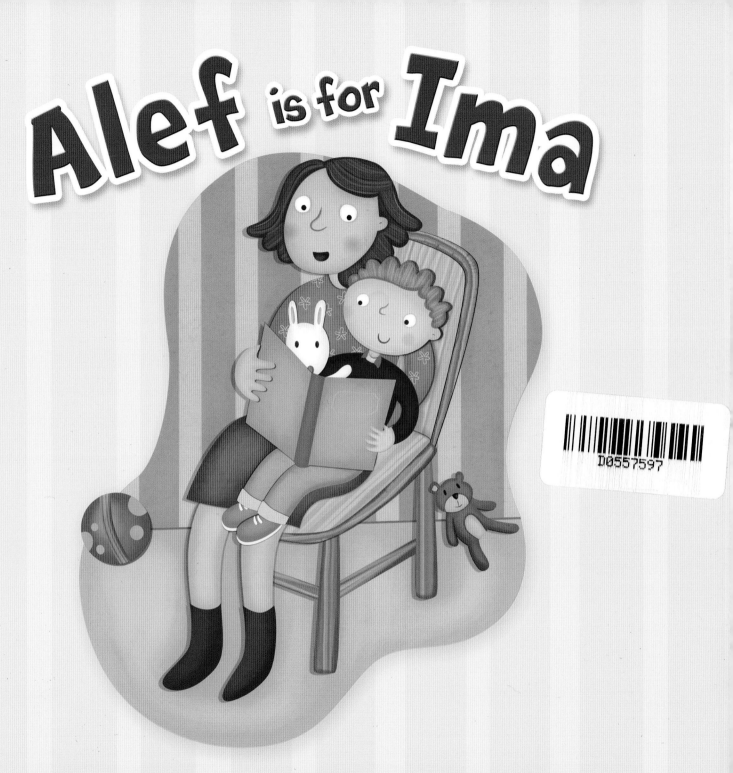

Rebecca Kafka   Illustrated by Constanza Basaluzzo

KAR-BEN
PUBLISHING

אִמָּא
Ima
Mother

אוֹר
Or
Light

אֶחָד
Echad
One

אַמְבַּטְיָה

Ambatyah

Bath

אֳנִיָּה

Oniyah

Boat

אוֹרְחִים
Orchim
Guests

אֲרוּחָה

Aruchah
Meal

אֵשׁ
Aish
Fire

אֹשֶׁר
Osher
Happiness

אַף

Af

Nose

אֲנִי אוֹהֶבֶת אוֹתְךָ!

Ani ohevet otchah!
I love you!

אֲנִי אוֹהֵב אוֹתְךָ!
Ani ohev otchah!
I love you!

אֹכֶל
Ochel
Food

אָדֹם

Adom

Red

אָבִיב

Aviv

Spring

אֲבַטִיחַ

Avatiach

Watermelon

אוטו
Auto
Car

אָרוֹן

Aron

Closet

אַרְיֵה

Aryeh

Lion

אֹזֶן

Ozen

Ear

אַבָּא

Abba
Father

This PJ BOOK belongs to

PJ Library®

JEWISH BEDTIME STORIES and SONGS

KAR-BEN PUBLISHING
A division of Lerner Publishing Group, Inc.
241 First Avenue North
Minneapolis, MN 55401 U.S.A.
1-800-4-KARBEN

Website address: www.karben.com

Main body text set in Slappy Inline.
Typeface provided by T26.

Library of Congress Cataloging-in-Publication Data

Kafka, Rebecca.
    Alef is for Abba / by Rebecca Kafka ; Illustrated by Constanza Basaluzzo.
       pages   cm
    Summary: "A young family interacts doing everyday tasks like going to the store, getting dressed and eating while Hebrew words are revealed to the reader"—Provided by publisher.
    ISBN 978–1–4677–2156–1 (lib. bdg. : alk. paper)
    ISBN 978–1–4677–4667–0 (eBook)
    [1. Family life—Fiction. 2. Vocabulary. 3. Hebrew language materials—Bilingual.]
  I. Basaluzzo, Constanza, illustrator. II. Title.
  PZ40.K33A44 2015
  [E]—dc23   2013021732

Manufactured in Hong Kong
1 – PN – 6/1/14

091425K1

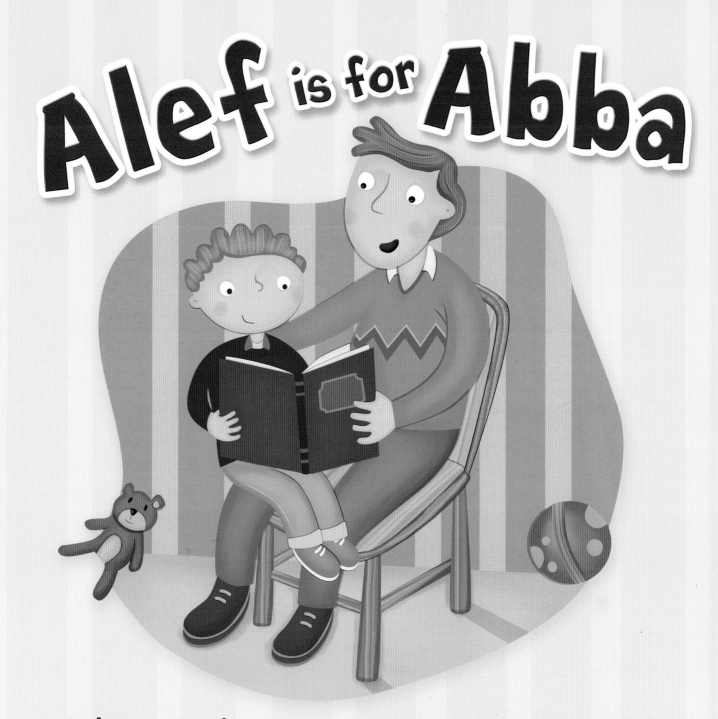

Alef is for Abba

Rebecca Kafka   Illustrated by Constanza Basaluzzo

KAR-BEN
PUBLISHING